ISBN 0-86163-692-9

This edition first published 1993
Second impression 1994

Published by Award Publications Limited,
1st Floor, Goodyear House,
52-56 Osnaburgh Street, London NW1 3NS

Printed in Singapore

HELLO
BRER RABBIT

Illustrated
by
RENE CLOKE

AWARD PUBLICATIONS LIMITED

THE GREAT RACE

Brer Rabbit was very good at playing tricks on the other animals but sometimes they were too clever for him.

Brer Terrapin was walking slowly along the road one day when he met Brer Rabbit.

"Hello slow-coach!" laughed Brer Rabbit. "You look as though you're in a hurry!"

Brer Terrapin felt annoyed.

"I may be slow on land," he replied, "but I'm a good swimmer."

Brer Rabbit knew that although Brer Terrapin could swim, he was no quicker in the water than he was on the land.

"We'll have a race," said Brer Rabbit.
"I'll go by land and you can swim
in the river."
Brer Terrapin agreed to this,
so all the animals helped
them to measure
five miles along
the river path,
marking each mile
with a post.

Early next morning, Brer Terrapin put his wife and each of his four children at a post, then hid himself at the winning post.

All the terrapins looked the same. so when Mrs Terrapin dived into the water at the words "Ready? Go!" Brer Rabbit thought that she was Brer Terrapin.

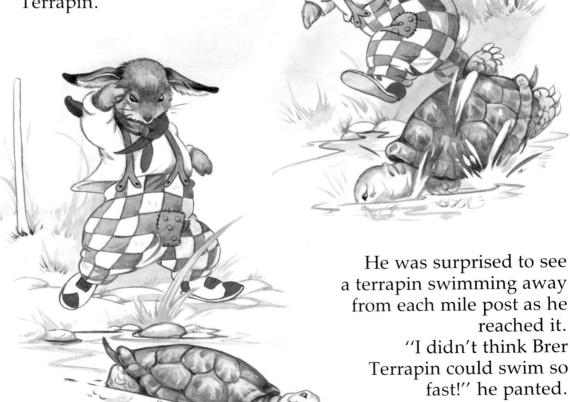

He was surprised to see a terrapin swimming away from each mile post as he reached it. "I didn't think Brer Terrapin could swim so fast!" he panted.

When he reached the winning
post, he was amazed to find
Brer Terrapin already there.
"I'm tired of waiting
for you," laughed the
terrapin, "did you lose
your way?"

Brer Rabbit simply couldn't
understand what had happened.
How had Brer Terrapin
arrived first at the winning
post when he was such a
slow coach?
But he was careful not
to laugh at the terrapin
next time he met him
crawling along.

BRER FOX GOES HUNTING

Brer Fox went hunting one day and came back in the evening with a heavy bag over his shoulder. He didn't know that Brer Rabbit was watching him from the bushes.

"There must be something good in that bag," said Brer Rabbit to himself. "Perhaps I can trick Brer Fox into giving some of it to me; I would like a tasty morsel for my supper."

He ran on ahead of Brer Fox, pulled off his clothes and lay down in the middle of the road, pretending to be dead.

Along came Brer Fox and turned over the rabbit with his stick.

"Here's a fine fat rabbit," he declared, "and he seems to be dead. A pity I can't take him but I've as much as I can carry already," and off he went.

As soon as Brer Fox was out of sight, Brer Rabbit jumped up and, running through the woods, he lay down again in the road where he knew Brer Fox would find him.

''Well, this is a surprise,'' said Brer Fox, looking at the rabbit. ''Another dead rabbit just waiting to be picked up. I think I'll leave my bag here and go back and collect the other one. It seems silly not to have them both. I'll bring another bag to put them in.''

Off went Brer Fox
thinking of the fine
feast he would have;
a bagful of birds
and animals, and two
fat rabbits as well.

"Just as I planned," laughed Brer
Rabbit jumping up and putting on his
clothes as soon as Brer Fox had
disappeared down the road.
He snatched up the bag
and trotted home with it.
"Tricked again!" growled Brer Fox
when he discovered that the two
dead rabbits had vanished
as well as his bag and he
had to go home without
any supper.

HOW BRER RABBIT LOST HIS TAIL

Many years ago, Brer Rabbit had a long bushy tail rather like a squirrels; he was very proud of it and used to shake it as he walked.

One bright winter morning he met Brer Fox walking along carrying a string of fine fish.

"Those look good," said Brer Rabbit, "where did you catch them?"

"I caught them down in the river," answered Brer Fox. "There are plenty there."

"How did you catch them?" asked Brer Rabbit.

Brer Fox sat down on a log and tried to think for a moment how he could play a trick on Brer Rabbit.

"All you have to do," he said, "is to drop your tail into the water in the evening, and when you draw it up in the morning, it will be covered with fish."

"It sounds easy," thought Brer Rabbit.

So, that evening he put on his big warm coat and muffler, packed a basket of food and a hot drink, and set off to fish.

He sat on a big stone in the river and let his tail down into the water.

It was very, very cold and by morning poor Brer Rabbit felt quite frozen.

"I must be catching a fine lot of fish," he said to cheer himself up.

But when he tried to pull
his tail out of the water, he
found that it had frozen and
as he got up, it snapped off!
"Well, that was a trick,"
moaned poor Brer Rabbit
looking at his stump of
fluffy tail, "and no fish!"

And that is why
rabbits now have
little bob tails.

BRER RABBIT AND BRER BEAR

Brer Rabbit was very fond of green peas and lettuces, and when he found them growing in Brer Fox's garden, he crawled through the fence every day and had a good feast.

"I must set a trap," said Brer Fox, "someone is stealing my green peas and lettuces."

So he made a cunning trap by bending down a young tree just by the hole in the fence. He tied a rope to a high branch with a slip-knot at the end, then he fixed this on to a stick.

Next time Brer Rabbit
crept through the fence,
he knocked the stick away,
the rope caught him round
the legs and the tree sprang
back with Brer Rabbit
dangling in the air.

"Oh, dear!" he cried.
"I'm properly caught now!"

Just then, Brer Bear
came along.

"What are you doing
up there?" he asked.

"Making a pound a minute!" answered Brer Rabbit. "Brer Fox pays me to hang here and frighten the crows off his green peas and lettuces. But I'm very busy at present so, if you would like the job, you can take my place."

So Brer Bear helped Brer Rabbit down from the tree and fastened himself to a stronger part of the branch while Brer Rabbit ran away home with as much green stuff as he could carry.

"Ha! ha!" cried Brer Fox running from his house with a big stick. "So you're the thief who has been stealing my green peas and lettuces! Nicely caught Brer Bear!"

And poor Brer Bear got the punishment which should have been for Brer Rabbit.

"It's not always the biggest people who have the best brains," laughed Brer Rabbit as he enjoyed a meal of green peas and lettuces.